come along, kitten

To Joan Hauprich, with many thanks, for being
such a caring friend and delightful companion—J. R.

To the adorable Dylan Forrest with love—S. W.

SIMON & SCHUSTER BOOKS FOR YOUNG READERS
An imprint of Simon & Schuster Children's Publishing Division
1230 Avenue of the Americas, New York, New York 10020

SIMON & SCHUSTER BOOKS FOR YOUNG READERS is a trademark of Simon & Schuster.

Book design by Greg Stadnyk
The text for this book is set in Usherwood.
The illustrations are rendered in watercolor and colored pencil.
Manufactured in Mexico
2 4 6 8 10 9 7 5 3 1

Library of Congress Cataloging-in-Publication Data
Ryder, Joanne.
Come Along, Kitten / by Joanne Ryder ; illustrated by Susan Winter.
p. cm.
Summary: A kitten explores a garden and discovers its many delights.
ISBN 0-689-83164-1
[1. Cats—Fiction. 2. Animals—Infancy—Fiction. 3. Gardens—Fiction. 4 Stories in rhyme.] I. Winter, Susan, ill. II. Title.
PZ8.3.R9595 Ki 2003
[E]—dc21
2001020953

come along, kitten

By **Joanne Ryder** Illustrated by **Susan Winter**

Simon & Schuster Books for Young Readers
New York   London   Toronto   Sydney   Singapore

Come along, kitten,
come follow me.

I know of a place
I'd like you to see.

You don't want to follow?
Then I'll follow you.

It's fun to explore
a place that is new.

Run along, kitten,
eager and free;

you circle the birdbath
and race bumblebee.

You listen to mice songs
my old ears don't hear,

and sniff every hidey-hole
without any fear.
Be brave, daring kitten—
just know I am near.

Race along, kitten,
quick as can be,

you leap over cabbages
and nibble a pea.

You catch every leaf
the wind blows your way.

On cushions of moss,
you tumble and play.

Be happy, bright kitten.
Enjoy this fine day.

Dash along, kitten,
wild as can be,
you pounce after cricket
who leaps straight at *me*!

You climb into bushes,
and hidden from view,

you call to the world
with a loud, proud, "MEW MEW."

Be careful, dear kitten,
I care about you.

My little kitten,
wandering free,
may you go where you wish
and then . . .

come home with me!